# TIME TOGETHER

## Me and Dad

BY MARIA CATHERINE

ILLUSTRATED BY PASCAL CAMPION

THIS BOOK BELONGS TO:

- - - - - - - - - - - - - - - - - - - - - - - - - - - - - - - - - - - - - - - - - - - - - - - - - - - - - - - - - - - - - - - - - - -

Favourite song time

Colourful family portrait time

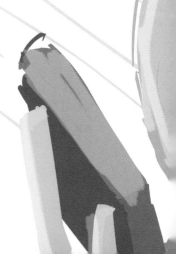

Sneaky hide and seek time

Fancy tea party time

# Fairy tale time

# Biscuit baking time

# Bear hug time

Quiet talking time

# Sky-high building time

Wild ride time

Dog walking time

Falling leaves time

# Shiny smile time

# Sweet dream time

Raintree is an imprint of Capstone Global Library Limited, a
company incorporated in England and Wales having its registered
office at 7 Pilgrim Street, London, EC4V 6LB – Registered
company number: 6695582

www.raintreepublishers.co.uk
myorders@raintreepublishers.co.uk

Copyright © 2014 Picture Window Books
First published in the United Kingdom in 2014
The moral rights of the proprietor have been asserted.

ISBN 978 1 406 27570 4
Printed in China by Nordica.
1013/CA21301928
17  16  15  14  13
10 9 8 7 6 5 4 3 2 1

British Library Cataloguing in Publication Data
A full catalogue record for this book is available from the British
Library.

Concept by: Kay Fraser and Christianne Jones
Designer: K. Fraser

Photo credits: Shutterstock